Visit us on the Web!
Seussville.com
rhcbooks.com

Educators and librarians, for a variety of teaching tools, visit us at RHTeachersLibrarians.com

Library of Congress Cataloging-in-Publication Data is available upon request.
ISBN 978-0-593-70627-5 (trade) — ISBN 978-0-593-70628-2 (lib. bdg.)
PRINTED IN THE UNITED STATES OF AMERICA
10 9 8 7 6 5 4 3
First Edition

Random House Children's Books supports the First Amendment and celebrates the right to read.

IF I DROVE
AN ICE CREAM
TRUCK

by **the Cat in the Hat**
with a little help from **Alastair Heim**
illustrated by **Tom Brannon**

BEGINNER BOOKS®
A Division of Random House

I just took a stroll
and am happy to say
that today is a bright,
sunny, SUMMERY day.

And as you all know,
when the weather is sunny,
we MUST play outside
and have fun that is funny!

And, while we are playing,
we MIGHT be in luck
and hear the sweet jingle
of the ice cream truck!

And when that truck stops
on the side of the street,
our tummies will really
be in for a treat!

If I drove an ice cream truck,

OH, GOODNESS ME!

Imagine how COOL

of a thing THAT would be. . . .

The very first thing
that I think I would do
is build my own truck
with a helper or two.

To start, we would find
the right ice cream truck parts
and load them all up
in these part-hauling carts.

We would roll them all down
to our truck factory,
to make the most ICE CREAM-Y
truck you would see.

And then, we would build!
We would build!
Build!
Build!
Build!

Till the tires were filled
and the freezers were chilled . . .

. . . and all of the MALTERS
and SLUSHERS and SHAKERS,
QUADRUPLE SCOOP-SCOOPERS
and FIZZY FLOAT MAKERS,
and ICE CREAM CONE CONERS
and cups by the cases
were loaded aboard
and all put in their places.

CUPS

CUPS

From Sunday through Friday,
and Saturday, too,
my ice cream truck crew
would create something new—
a tasty new treat
for EACH day of the week,
delightful, delicious,
and sweetly unique.

On Sunday, our sundaes
would come triple-dipped
and topped with whipped cream
that was triple-flip-whipped.

And just when you thought
that your treat was complete,
my crew would do something
that is really quite neat.

Thing One would go up
on a tall SPRINKLE THROWER,
while lower, Thing Two
would fly a SPRINKLE BLOWER
to make sure the sprinkles
float down a bit slower.

While plenty would stick
to the sundaes like glue,
a LOT of the sprinkles
would rain down on YOU!

On Monday, the flavors
of malts we would make
would number one hundred
and three, give or take.

The malts we would mix

would be served up with love . . .

. . . and pitched through the air
as you held out your glove.

On Tuesday, our truck
would pull up to the pool
and serve you a treat
that was SLUSH-FULLY cool.

Our slushies, you see,
would be served extra chilly.
No, really! So cold,
it would be kind of silly . . .

. . . so chilly, in fact,
if you spilled just ONE drop,
the pool would freeze up!
You could SKATE on the top!

On Wednesday, prepare
for our scoop-stacking game.
UP-UP-UP with the scoops
is its fun, fun, fun name!

Whoever can stack
the most scoops in an hour
and make the most eye-popping
ice cream scoop tower
would get an award
for their ice cream skyscraper—
and EVEN a spot
in the local newspaper!

On Thursday, at night,
when the sky is all dark,
my ice cream truck crew
would be parked in the park
to serve up some GLOW CONES.
And just so you know,
our glow cones are snow cones
but BETTER . . . they glow!

Then early on Friday
my crew would use things
like paintbrushes, hammers,
and streamers on strings
to add decorations
to all of these boats
and turn every one
into FLOAT-MAKING FLOATS.

My sweet fleet of fancy
new floats would be made
to serve ice cream floats
at an ICE CREAM PARADE!

Around and around,
we would drive 'round the block—
from eight in the morning
till seven o'clock—
and load up your cups
on our ICE CREAM CONVEYORS,
then fill them with fizz from our
SODA-POP SPRAYERS.

When Saturday came,
we would drive to the lake
to kick up our feet
for a well-deserved break
and serve up some self-serving
SHAKE-A-LOT SHAKES.

If I drove an ice cream truck,
life would be sweet,
delivering treats
that are SO nice to eat!

Just THINK of the smiles
we could serve up for you,
from Monday through Sunday,
the whole summer through.

Plus, SCOOPFULS of fun
with a cherry on top . . .

. . . should YOUR neighborhood be
my very first stop?